THE
Worst Princess

For Guinevere, Niamh, Emelia, Annabel, Esther, Elise, Esme, Martha, Orla, and rebel princesses everywhere
—A.K.

For Freya and Molly
—S.O.

Text copyright © 2012 by Anna Kemp
Cover art and interior illustrations copyright © 2012 by Sara Ogilvie

Visit us on the Web! randomhouse.com/kids

Educators and librarians, for a variety of teaching tools, visit us at RHTeachersLibrarians.com

Library of Congress Cataloging-in-Publication Data
Kemp, Anna.
The worst princess / by Anna Kemp & Sara Ogilvie. — 1st American ed.
p.   cm.
Summary: Lonely Princess Sue longs to leave her castle tower, but when
her prince finally rescues her, she realizes she is destined for a less
traditional partner.
ISBN 978-0-385-37125-4 (trade) — ISBN 978-0-375-98176-0 (ebook)
[1. Stories in rhyme. 2. Princesses—Fiction. 3. Princes—Fiction. 4. Sex
role—Fiction. 5. Dragons—Fiction.] I. Ogilvie, Sara, ill. II. Title.
PZ8.3.K337Wor 2014 [E]—dc23   2012040907

MANUFACTURED IN CHINA

10 9 8 7 6 5 4 3 2 1

First American Edition 2014

THE Worst Princess

Anna Kemp ◆ Sara Ogilvie

Random House 🏠 New York

Once upon a time, in a tower near you, lived a lonely princess—the Princess Sue.

"Someday," she sighed, "my prince will come,
but I wish he'd move his royal bum.
I've waited for a hundred years.
I'm getting stiff. I'm bored to tears."

"I've read the books,
I know the score,
I've grown my braids
down to the floor.
I really need to get some air,
to see the world
and cut my hair."

Then . . .

. . . just as Sue was about to scream,
a prince appeared. 'Twas like a dream.
"Oh, Princess, pretty as a pea!
I've journeyed far to rescue thee."

"I fought, I won,

I shocked, I awed."

"You should have seen me swing my sword.
I've slain all kinds of vicious foe. . . ."

"That's fab," said Sue. "Now can we go?
Your true love's kiss should do the trick,
so pucker up and kiss me quick!"

They charged off on a dashing steed.
"Whoopee!" cried Sue. "At last! I'm freed!
Today I start my happy end!"

But then she saw around the bend. . . .

"Where are we going, my prince, my love?"
"Back to my castle, turtledove.
My perfect peach, my precious flower,
you have a penthouse in the tower."

"I'd rather ride a horse," said Sue,
"and do all kinds of fun stuff too!"

"Too bad," said Prince. "You know the rules. Didn't you listen at Princess School?"

"It's me who wears the armor here,
and you wear dresses. Are we clear?

Just smile a lot and twist your curls.
Dragon-bashing's not for girls."

Alone in her tower, Sue started to spit,
"What a disaster. My prince is a twit!"
Then in the skies she suddenly spied . . .

...a fearsome dragon with flashing eyes.

Sue didn't run, she had no fear.
Instead, she had a bright idea.

"Hey, you," she called, "with the scary claws!
Fancy some tea for your fiery jaws?"
"Ooh, yes," said Dragon. "What a relief.
That pesky prince is giving me grief."

"Me too," said Sue. "The sneaky rascal
has locked me in this stupid castle."

"The twit!" gasped Dragon. "That just won't do!
We need to teach him a thing or two!"
The dragon sniffed some nasal spray . . .

. . . then blew the tower clean away!

"Princess Sue! That's quite enough!"
The prince was back, and in a huff.
"Where's your tower? Just look at your dress!
You really are the worst princess."

"Also, Susan, beg your pardon,
why's there a dragon in my garden?"

"Perhaps I am the worst princess," laughed Princess Sue. "My hair's a mess, my tower's a wreck, but I don't care. I've booked a flight with Dragon-Air!"

The dragon sniffed, then with two snorts . . .

. . . set alight the princely shorts!

From that day on, the newfound friends
toured the land from end to end . . .

making mischief left and right . . .

for royal twits and naughty knights.

"You know," said Sue as they drank their tea,
"we're a great team, you and me."
The dragon's belly shook with laughter.

And they both lived happily ever after.